The Read-Aloud Treasury

The Read-Aloud Treasury

COMPILED BY
JOANNA COLE AND
STEPHANIE CALMENSON

ILLUSTRATED BY
ANN SCHWENINGER

Doubleday New York

For Barbara Greenman

Art Direction by Diana Klemin
Book Design by Marilyn Schulman

Library of Congress Cataloging-in-Publication Data

The Read-aloud treasury.

Includes index.
Summary: An illustrated collection of classic and modern nursery rhymes, poems,
stories, and activity games for preschoolers through age five.
1. Children's literature. [1. Literature–Collections] I. Cole, Joanna. II.
Calmenson, Stephanie. III. Schweninger, Ann, ill.
PZ5.R1984   1988   808.8′99282   86-24138
ISBN 0-385-18560-X

CONTENTS

Poems

Stories

Play and Learn

READING WITH YOUR CHILD

THE READ-ALOUD TREASURY is a collection of children's literature that you can begin reading to your child from babyhood and continue enjoying through the early school years.

The book begins with nursery rhymes and poems. The sounds and rhythms of words are what attract young children to poetry. Reading a poem is almost like singing a song: *Do the baby cake – walk/A one-step, a two-step/A wobble & a bobble in the knee.* Try asking your child to recite some of the poems and rhymes along with you.

Then there are stories. A toddler may not agree that a story needs to be read from beginning to end. Sometimes it is best just to look at the pictures and ask your child to "point to the cat" or "find the yellow truck." Whenever your child seems ready, you can begin to read whole stories. Be prepared for your child to become attached to a favorite one and ask for it again and again over days or weeks. For many children this is an important part of mastering the written word.

Finally there is a chapter called "Play and Learn," which includes material that will help develop specific reading skills. There is a rebus, which offers the chance to "read" pictures the way words will be read later on, and a wordless story, so that your child can tell you what is happening in her own words.

Even after your child has learned to read on his own, the pleasure of reading aloud continues because hearing again and again the richness and rhythms of literature expands his imagination. We hope THE READ-ALOUD TREASURY is a book that you and your child will enjoy over many years to come.

Joanna Cole and Stephanie Calmenson

Nursery Rhymes

PAT-A-CAKE, PAT-A-CAKE

Pat-a-cake, pat-a-cake, baker's man!
   Bake me a cake as fast as you can;
Pat it and prick it and mark it with "B"
   And put it in the oven for baby and me.

BROW, BROW, BRINKIE

Brow, brow, brinkie,
Eye, eye, winkie,
Mouth, mouth, merry,
Cheek, cheek, cherry,
Chin-chopper, chin-chopper.

THIS LITTLE PIG WENT TO MARKET

This little pig went to market;
This little pig stayed home;
This little pig had roast beef;
This little pig had none;
This little pig cried,
"Wee, wee, wee!"
All the way home.

HUMPTY DUMPTY

Humpty Dumpty sat on a wall,
Humpty Dumpty had a great fall.
　　All the king's horses,
　　And all the king's men
Couldn't put Humpty together again.

THE OLD WOMAN WHO LIVED IN A SHOE

There was an old woman who lived
    in a shoe.
She had so many children she
    didn't know what to do.
She gave them some broth without
    any bread.
She spanked them all soundly and
    put them to bed.

RUB-A-DUB-DUB

Rub-a-dub-dub,
Three men in a tub;
And who do you think they be?
The butcher, the baker,
The candlestick-maker;
Turn 'em out, knaves all three!

ONE, TWO, BUCKLE MY SHOE

One, two,
Buckle my shoe;
Three, four,
Shut the door;
Five, six,
Pick up sticks;
Seven, eight,
Lay them straight;
Nine, ten,
A good, fat hen;
Eleven, twelve,
Dig and delve;
Thirteen, fourteen,
Maids a-courting;
Fifteen, sixteen,
Maids in the kitchen;
Seventeen, eighteen,
Maids a-waiting;
Nineteen, twenty,
My plate's empty.

LADYBIRD, LADYBIRD

Ladybird, ladybird, fly away home!
 Your house is on fire, your children all gone;
All but one, and her name is Ann,
 And she crept under the pudding pan.

OLD KING COLE

Old King Cole was a merry old soul,
 And a merry old soul was he.
He called for his pipe, he called for his bowl,
 And he called for his fiddlers three.

I SAW A SHIP A-SAILING

I saw a ship a-sailing,
A-sailing on the sea;
And, oh! it was all laden
With pretty things for thee!

There were comfits in the cabin,
And apples in the hold;
The sails were made of silk,
And the masts were made of gold.

The four-and-twenty sailors
That stood between the decks,
Were four-and-twenty white mice
With chains about their necks.

The captain was a duck,
With a packet on his back;
And when the ship began to move,
The captain said, "Quack! Quack!"

RIDE A COCK-HORSE

Ride a cock-horse to Banbury Cross,
To see a fine lady upon a white horse.
Rings on her fingers, and bells on her toes,
She shall have music wherever she goes.

BAA, BAA, BLACK SHEEP

Baa, baa, black sheep, have you any wool?
Yes, sir, yes, sir, three bags full:
One for my master, one for my dame,
And one for the little boy that lives down the lane.

DIDDLETY, DIDDLETY, DUMPTY

Diddlety, diddlety, dumpty,
The cat ran up a plum tree;
    Half a crown
    To fetch her down,
Diddlety, diddlety, dumpty.

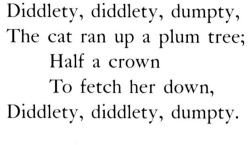

WHERE HAS MY LITTLE DOG GONE?

Where, oh, where has my little dog gone?
Oh, where, oh, where can he be?
With his tail cut short, and his ears cut long—
Oh, where, oh, where can he be?

THREE LITTLE KITTENS

Three little kittens lost their mittens,
    and they began to cry,
"Oh, mother dear, we sadly fear
    Our mittens we have lost!"

"What! lost your mittens,
    you naughty kittens!
Then you shall have no pie."
    "Meow, meow, meow!"

The three little kittens found their mittens,
    and they began to cry,
"Oh! mother dear, see here, see here,
    Our mittens we have found."

"What! found your mittens,
    you good little kittens,
Then you shall have some pie."
    "Purr, purr, purr."

MARY HAD A LITTLE LAMB

Mary had a little lamb,
    Its fleece was white as snow;
And everywhere that Mary went
    The lamb was sure to go.

He followed her to school one day,
    Which was against the rule;
It made the children laugh and play
    To see a lamb at school.

LITTLE BOY BLUE

Little Boy Blue,
    Come blow your horn,
The sheep's in the meadow,
    The cow's in the corn;
But where is the boy
    Who looks after the sheep?
He's under a haycock,
    Fast asleep.
Will you wake him?
    No, not I,
For if I do,
    He's sure to cry.

THERE WAS A CROOKED MAN

There was a crooked man, and he
    walked a crooked mile,
He found a crooked sixpence
    beside a crooked stile;
He bought a crooked cat,
    which caught a crooked mouse,
And they all lived together
    in a little crooked house.

THE OLD WOMAN WHO LIVED
UNDER A HILL

There was an old woman
Lived under a hill,
And if she's not gone
She lives there still.

LITTLE BO PEEP

Little Bo Peep has lost her sheep,
And can't tell where to find them;
Leave them alone, and they'll come home,
Wagging their tails behind them.

RAIN, RAIN, GO AWAY

Rain, rain, go away,
Come again another day;
Little Johnny wants to play.

JACK BE NIMBLE

Jack be nimble,
Jack be quick,
Jack jump over the candlestick.

JACK AND JILL

Jack and Jill went up the hill,
To fetch a pail of water;
Jack fell down, and broke his crown,
And Jill came tumbling after.

THERE WAS A BEE

There was a bee
    Sat on a wall;
He said he could hum,
    And that was all.

RING AROUND THE ROSIE

Ring around the rosie,
A pocketful of posies,
Ashes, ashes,
All fall down!

MISTRESS MARY, QUITE CONTRARY

Mistress Mary, quite contrary,
    How does your garden grow?
With silver bells and cockle shells
    And pretty maids all in a row.

SEESAW, MARGERY DAW

Seesaw, Margery Daw,
    Jackey shall have a new master;
He shall have but a penny a day,
    Because he can't work any faster.

SING A SONG OF SIXPENCE

Sing a song of sixpence,
    a pocket full of rye;
Four-and-twenty blackbirds
    baked in a pie!
When the pie was opened
    the birds began to sing;
Wasn't that a dainty dish
    to set before the King?

The King was in the countinghouse,
    counting out his money;
The Queen was in the parlor,
    eating bread and honey.
The maid was in the garden,
    hanging out the clothes;
When down came a blackbird
    and snapped off her nose.

Poems

HOPPITY

Christopher Robin goes
Hoppity, hoppity,
Hoppity, hoppity, hop.
Whenever I tell him
Politely to stop it, he
Says he can't possibly stop.
If he stopped hopping, he couldn't go anywhere,
Poor little Christopher
Couldn't go anywhere . . .
That's why he *always* goes
Hoppity, hoppity,
Hoppity,
Hoppity,
Hop.

A. A. Milne

DO THE BABY CAKE-WALK

Do the baby cake-walk
A one-step, a two-step
A wobble & a bobble in the knee,
With a toe heel toe
And a giddy-go-round you go
Won't you do the baby cake-walk
For me?

Clyde Watson

BABY'S DRINKING SONG

Sip a little
Sup a little
From your little
Cup a little
Sup a little
Sip a little
Put it to your
Lip a little
Tip a little
Tap a little
Not into your
Lap or it'll
Drip a little
Drop a little
On the table
Top a little.

James Kirkup

THE POPCORN HOP

Put your popcorn
in a pot.
Wait till it gets
really hot.
When you start to
feel the heat,
Listen for the
popcorn beat:
Pop-pop-POP-pop,
pop-pop-POP!
Come and do the
popcorn hop!

Stephanie Calmenson

THREE GUESTS

I had a little tea-party,
This afternoon at three;
    'Twas very small,
    Three guests in all,
Just I, myself, and me.

Myself ate up the sandwiches,
While I drank up the tea,
    'Twas also I
    Who ate the pie
And passed the cake to me.

Jessica Nelson North

AFTER A BATH

After my bath
I try, try, try
to wipe myself
till I'm dry, dry, dry.

Hands to wipe
and fingers and toes
and two wet legs
and a shiny nose.

Just think how much
less time I'd take
if I were a dog
and could shake, shake, shake.

Aileen Fisher

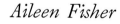

LITTLE PICTURES

Little pictures
Hang above me.
Pictures of the folks
Who love me.
Mom and Dad
and Uncle Jack,
They love me . . .
I love them back.

Arnold Lobel

FIRST SNOW

Snow makes whiteness where it falls.
The bushes look like popcorn-balls.
And places where I always play,
Look like somewhere else today.

Marie Louise Allen

44

THE MITTEN SONG

"Thumbs in the thumb-place,
Fingers all together!"
This is the song
We sing in mitten-weather.
When it is cold,
It doesn't matter whether
Mittens are wool,
Or made of finest leather.
This is the song
We sing in mitten-weather:
"Thumbs in the thumb-place,
Fingers all together!"

Marie Louise Allen

from
THE UMBRELLA BRIGADE

Oh, let it rain
Tree-toads and frogs,
Muskets and pitchforks,
Kittens and dogs!
Dash away! plash away!
Who is afraid?
Here we go,
The Umbrella Brigade!

Laura E. Richards

RAIN

The rain is raining all around,
It falls on field and tree,
It rains on the umbrellas here,
And on the ships at sea.

Robert Louis Stevenson

MUD

I like mud.
      I like it on my clothes.
I like it on my fingers.
      I like it in my toes.

Dirt's pretty ordinary
      And dust's a dud.
For a really good mess-up
      I like mud.

John Smith

THE MERRY-GO-ROUND

Come for a ride
    On the merry-go-round.
The merry-go,
    Merry-go-round!

Merry-go-high
    And merry-go-low.
Giddy-up horse!
    Away we go!

Merry-go-up
    And merry-go-down.
Merry-go-round
    And round and round!

Stephanie Calmenson

PLAY

Come play with me said the sun,
come play with me said the earth,
come play with me said the sky.
What shall we play said I?

Let's fly a kite said the sun,
stand on me said the earth,
I'll bring the wind said the sky,
I'll hold the string said I.

Frank Asch

from
THE MAN WHO SANG THE SILLIES

Oh, The Sillies are the sweetest that I know:
    They have grins as big as tickles,
    They have titters up their sleeves,
    They make faces dill as pickles,
    And they spin like autumn leaves.
    They have cheeks as red as cherry,
    And they're always losing shoes,
    But they're very very very very
    Easy to amuse.
    You need only call their names
    And they start their giggle games.
    They go scramble-clatter-thump across the floor.
    They go tumble-flopping in and out the door.
    What a screech and clatter! What a roar!
But I always think when it comes time to go
That The Sillies are the sweetest that I know.

Yes, The Sillies are the sweetest that I know.
    They're a nuisance, they're a bother.
    They're an everlasting noise.
    Sillies act like one another.
    Sillies act like girls and boys.
    Sillies think it's necessary
    Not to like what they are fed.
    They are very very very very
    Hard to put to bed.
    You need only say "Bedtime . . ."
    And they run away and climb
    Up the chimney, up a moonbeam, out of sight.
    Till they're caught and snuggled tight.
    Then they yawn and say "Goodnight . . . ."
    And their voices are so soft away and slow,
That I have to think when it comes time to go
That The Luckies are The Happies,
    and The Happies are The Sillies,
And The Sillies are the sweetest that I know.

John Ciardi

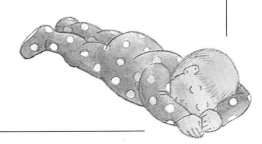

BARNYARD CHAT

"Honk, honk."
"Oink, oink."
"Meow, meow."
"Neigh."

"Cluck, cluck."
"Woof, woof."
"Gobble, gobble."
"Bray!"

"Baa, baa."
"Hoot, hoot."
"Cackle, cackle."
"Moo."

"Quack, quack."
"Peep, peep."
"Cock-a-doodle-doo!"

Stephanie Calmenson

TODAY IS A DAY TO CROW ABOUT

Today is a day to crow about,
it's a crowable sort of day,
for the crows have frightened the scarecrow,
and the scarecrow is running away.

Jack Prelutsky

KITTENS

Our cat had kittens
weeks ago
when everything outside was snow.

So she stayed in
and kept them warm
and safe from all the clouds and storm.

But yesterday
when there was sun
she snuzzled on the smallest one

and turned it over
from beneath
and took its fur between her teeth

and carried it
outside to see
how nice a winter day can be

and then our dog
decided he
would help her take the other three

and one by one
they took them out
to see what sun is all about

so when they're grown
they'll always know
to never be afraid of snow.

Myra Cohn Livingston

MICE

I think mice
Are rather nice.

Their tails are long,
Their faces small,
They haven't any
Chins at all.
Their ears are pink,
Their teeth are white,
They run about
The house at night.
They nibble things
They shouldn't touch
And no one seems
To like them much.

But I think mice
Are nice.

Rose Fyleman

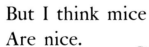

PLEASE!

Mouse, mouse,
Get out of my house!
Take your whiskers.
Take your cheese.
Get out of my house, mouse . . .
PLEASE!

What? You say you have nowhere to go?
You say it's cold out in the snow?

Mouse, mouse,
Come into the house.
Bring your whiskers.
Bring your cheese.
Come back in the house, mouse . . .
PLEASE.

Stephanie Calmenson

from
IT DOES *NOT* SAY MEOW
and Other Animal Riddle Rhymes

Can you finish each poem by guessing the animal?

Try it and see.

It has two feet,
No hands, two wings.
It can fly
In the sky.

Sometimes it chirps.
Sometimes it sings
The sweetest song
You ever heard.
Can you guess?
It is a . . .

bird

A short short tail.
A long long nose.
He uses for
A water hose.

Two great big ears.
Four great big feet.
A tiny peanut
Is a treat
                for him.

His name is El—
Oh no! I can't!
Now *you* tell *me:* An . . .

elephant

It's glad when you're glad,
Sad when you're sad,
Has a head you can pat,
But it is not a cat.
(It does *not* say *me-ow.*)
And it doesn't say moo,
So it is not a cow.

It says *woof* or *bow-wow.*
Does that sound like a frog?
No! It's a . . .

dog

It's busy as a bee.
It's buzzy as a bee.
Looks funny as a bee.
Makes honey like a bee.

It must be a . . .

bee

Beatrice Schenk de Regniers

from

A HOUSE IS A HOUSE FOR ME

A hill is a house for an ant, an ant.
A hive is a house for a bee.
A hole is house for a mole or a mouse
And a house is a house for me!

A garage is a house for a car or a truck.
A hangar's a house for a plane.
A dock or a slip is a house for a ship
And a terminal's house for a train.

The cooky jar's home to the cookies.
The breadbox is home to the bread.
My coat is a house for my body.
My hat is a house for my head.

A glove is a house for a hand, a hand.
A stocking's a house for a knee.
A shoe or a boot is a house for a foot
And a house is a house for me!

Mary Ann Hoberman

MY NAME IS . . .

My name is Sluggery-wuggery
My name is Worms-for-tea
My name is Swallow-the-table-leg
My name is Drink-the-Sea.
My name is I-eat-saucepans
My name is I-like-snails
My name is Grand-piano-George
My name is I-ride-whales.
My name is Jump-the-chimney
My name is Bite-my-knee
My name is Jiggery-pokery
And Riddle-me-ree, and ME.

Pauline Clarke

HELLO, HELLO, HELLO, SIR
(A Jump Rope Rhyme)

"Hello, hello, hello, sir,
Meet me at the grocer."
"No sir."
"Why sir?"
"Because I have a cold, sir."
"Where did you get your cold, sir?"
"At the North Pole, sir."
"What were you doing there, sir?"
"Counting polar bears, sir."
"Let me hear you sneeze, sir."
"Kachoo, kachoo, kachoo, sir."

Traditional

SPELLING LESSON

C-A-T.
That spells cat.
Mine eats too much,
So now he's - - - !

Stephanie Calmenson

WAY DOWN SOUTH

Way down South where bananas grow.
A grasshopper stepped on an elephant's toe.
The elephant said, with tears in his eyes,
"Pick on somebody your own size."

Traditional

FUZZY WUZZY

Fuzzy Wuzzy was a bear;
Fuzzy Wuzzy had no hair.
Fuzzy Wuzzy wasn't fuzzy,
Was he?

Traditional

THE SAILOR SONG

A sailor went to sea, sea, sea
To see what he could see, see, see.
But all that he could see, see, see,
Was the bottom of the deep blue sea, sea, sea!

Traditional

THE OWL AND THE PUSSY-CAT

The Owl and the Pussy-cat went to sea
    In a beautiful pea-green boat:
They took some honey, and plenty of money
    Wrapped up in a five-pound note.
The Owl looked up to the stars above,
    And sang to a small guitar,
"O lovely Pussy, O Pussy, my love,
    What a beautiful Pussy you are,
        You are,
        You are!
    What a beautiful Pussy you are!"

Pussy said to the Owl, "You elegant fowl,
How charmingly sweet you sing!
Oh! let us be married; too long we have tarried:
But what shall we do for a ring?"
They sailed away, for a year and a day,
To the land where the bong-tree grows;
And there in a wood a Piggy-wig stood,
With a ring at the end of his nose,
His nose,
His nose,
With a ring at the end of his nose.

"Dear Pig, are you willing to sell for one shilling
Your ring?" Said the Piggy, "I will."
So they took it away, and were married next day
By the turkey who lives on the hill.
They dined on mince and slices of quince,
Which they ate with a runcible spoon;
And hand in hand, on the edge of the sand,
They danced by the light of the moon,
The moon,
The moon,
They danced by the light of the moon.

Edward Lear

SLEEPY MOUSE

Sleepy mouse, sleepy mouse,
Going home to his little house.
He opens the door
With a jangle of keys,
And has a small supper
Of bread and cheese.
He climbs into bed,
And he turns out the light.
Now this little mouse
Is asleep for the night.

Joanna Cole

LITTLE BEAR
GOES TO THE MOON

by Else Holmelund Minarik
Pictures by Maurice Sendak

"I have a new space helmet.
I am going to the moon," said Little Bear to
Mother Bear.
"How?" asked Mother Bear.

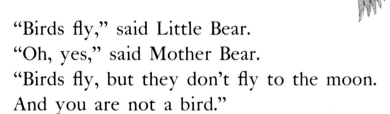

"I'm going to fly to the moon,"
said Little Bear.
"Fly!" said Mother Bear.
"You can't fly."

"Birds fly," said Little Bear.
"Oh, yes," said Mother Bear.
"Birds fly, but they don't fly to the moon.
And you are not a bird."

"Maybe some birds fly to the moon,
I don't know.
And maybe I can fly like a bird,"
said Little Bear.

"And maybe," said Mother Bear,
"You are a little fat bear cub
with no wings and no feathers.

"Maybe if you jump up
you will come down very fast,
with a big plop."

"Maybe," said Little Bear.
"But I'm going now.
Just look for me up in the sky."
"Be back for lunch," said Mother.

Little Bear thought.
I will jump from a good high spot,
far up into the sky,
and fly up, up, up.

I will be going too fast
to look at things,
so I will shut my eyes.

Little Bear climbed to the top of a little hill,
and climbed to the top of a little tree,
a very little tree on the little hill,
and shut his eyes and jumped.

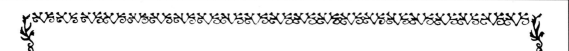

Down, down he came with a big plop,
and down the hill he tumbled.
Then he sat up and looked around.
"My, my," he said.
"Here I am on the moon.

"The moon looks just like the earth.
Well, well," said Little Bear.
"The trees here look just like our trees.
The birds look just like our birds.

"And look at this," he said.
"Here is a house that looks just like my house.
I'll go in and see what kind of bears live here.

"Look at that," said Little Bear.
"Something to eat is on the table.
It looks like a good lunch for a little bear."

Mother Bear came in and said,
"But who is this?
Are you a bear from Earth?"
"Oh, yes, I am," said Little Bear.
"I climbed a little hill,
and jumped from a little tree,
and flew here, just like the birds."

"Well," said Mother Bear.
"My little bear did the same thing.
He put on his space helmet and flew to Earth.
So I guess you can have his lunch."

Little Bear put his arms around Mother Bear.
He said, "Mother Bear, stop fooling.
You are my Mother Bear
and I am your Little Bear,
and we are on Earth, and you know it.
Now may I eat my lunch?"

"Yes," said Mother Bear,
"and then you will have your nap.
For you are my little bear,
and I know it."

THE THREE BILLY GOATS GRUFF

Once upon a time there were three billy goats who wanted to go up to the hillside to make themselves fat, and the name of all three was "Gruff."

On the way up was a bridge they had to cross; and under the bridge lived a great ugly Troll, with eyes as big as saucers and a nose as long as a poker.

So first of all came the youngest Billy Goat Gruff to cross the bridge.

"Trip, trap, trip, trap!" went the bridge.

"WHO'S THAT tripping over my bridge?" roared the Troll.

"Oh, it is only I, the tiniest Billy Goat Gruff; and I'm going up to the hillside to make myself fat," said the billy goat, in a small voice.

"Now, I'm coming to gobble you up," said the Troll.

"Oh no, don't take me. I'm too little," said the billy goat. "Wait a bit till the second Billy Goat Gruff comes. He's much bigger."

"Well, be off with you," said the Troll.

A little while after came the second Billy Goat Gruff to cross the bridge.

"TRIP, TRAP! TRIP, TRAP! TRIP, TRAP!" went the bridge.

"WHO'S THAT tripping over my bridge?" roared the Troll.

"Oh, it's the second Billy Goat Gruff, and I'm going up to the hillside to make myself fat," said the billy goat, who hadn't such a small voice.

"Now, I'm coming to gobble you up," said the Troll.

"Oh no, don't take me; wait a little till the third Billy Goat Gruff comes. He's much bigger."

"Very well, be off with you," said the Troll.

But just then up came the big Billy Goat Gruff.

"TRIP, TRAP! TRIP, TRAP! TRIP, TRAP!" went the bridge, for the billy goat was so heavy that the bridge creaked and groaned under him.

"WHO'S THAT tramping over my bridge?" roared the Troll.

"IT'S I! THE BIG BILLY GOAT GRUFF," said the billy goat, who had an ugly hoarse voice of his own.

"Now, I'm coming to gobble you up," roared the Troll.

"Well, come along! I've got two spears,
    And I'll poke your eyeballs out at your ears;
    I've got besides two great flat stones,
    And I'll crush you to bits, body and bones."

That was what the big billy goat said, and that is what the big billy goat did.

And after that he went up to the hillside. There the billy goats got so fat they were hardly able to walk home again; and if the fat hasn't fallen off them, why, they're still fat; and so—

Snip, snap, snout,
This tale's told out.

LITTLE RED RIDING HOOD

Once there was a little girl whom everyone loved. Her grandmother made her a red velvet hood, and it looked so nice that the little girl wore it every day. After that, everyone called her Little Red Riding Hood.

One day her mother said, "Little Red Riding Hood, take these cakes and honey to your grandmother. She is sick, and they will make her feel better. Go straight to Grandmother's house and do not go off the path and into the woods."

No sooner had Little Red Riding Hood set foot on the path in the woods when she met the wolf.

"Hello," said the wolf. "Where are you going so early?"

Little Red Riding Hood didn't know how dangerous it was to talk to a wolf, so she answered, "I am taking these cakes and honey to my grandmother, who is sick."

"Where does she live?" asked the wolf.

"In the woods near the three oak trees," answered Little Red Riding Hood politely.

The wolf thought to himself, "I will eat the grandmother and the little girl too!"

But to Little Red Riding Hood he said, "Why are you in such a hurry, little girl? Look at all the beautiful flowers growing around you."

"Grandmother *would* like a pretty bouquet," thought Little Red Riding Hood, and she left the path and began to pick flowers.

Meanwhile the wolf ran as fast as he could to the grandmother's house.

"Who is there?" called Grandmother.

"It is Little Red Riding Hood," said the wolf, making his voice as soft as he could.

"Lift the latch and come in," said the grandmother.

The wolf went in, and without a word, he swallowed the grandmother up in one gulp.

Then he put on her nightgown and nightcap and lay down in the bed.

After a while, Little Red Riding Hood came to the house. She was surprised to find the door open, and when she went in, she thought, "Why am I so frightened today? I'm usually so happy at Grandmother's house."

Then she went up to the bed. The grandmother had her cap pulled way down over her face, and she looked very strange.

"Grandmother, what big ears you have!"

"The better to hear you with, my dear."

"What big eyes you have!"

"The better to see you with, my dear."

"What big hands you have!"

"The better to hold you with, my dear."

"But Grandmother, what big teeth you have!"

94

"The better to eat you with, my dear!"
Then the wolf jumped out of bed and ate up Little Red Riding Hood.

Now the wolf was not hungry anymore, but he felt very sleepy. So he climbed back into bed and began to snore.

A hunter was passing by, and he thought, "How loudly the old woman is snoring! I'd better go in and see if she is all right."

So he stepped into the house and found the wolf.

"I've got you at last, you wicked fellow!" said the hunter, and started to kill the wolf. But then he thought, "Maybe the old woman is inside," and taking some scissors, he cut open the sleeping wolf's belly. Two snips—and the little girl popped out, saying, "Oh, it was so dark in there!"

Two more snips—out came the grandmother, and she was still alive too!

Little Red Riding Hood ran outside and got some big stones.

They put them in the wolf's belly and sewed him up. When he woke up, he tried to run away, but the stones were so heavy that he fell down dead.

Then the hunter took the wolf skin home, the grandmother ate the cakes and honey and soon felt better, and Little Red Riding Hood said to herself, "I will never again leave the path and run into the woods when Mother tells me not to!"

DINNER GUESTS
An African Folktale
retold by Stephanie Calmenson

One hot-hot day Turtle was walking home through the woods when he smelled delicious things cooking at Anansi the Spider's house. Now Turtle was tired and hungry from his long walk, so he knocked on Anansi's door.

Anansi was not happy to see Turtle standing there. He was just about to eat his dinner of fish and yams, and he wanted it all for himself. But Anansi knew that he must never turn a visitor away. So he said, "Greetings, Mr. Turtle. Won't you come in and share my dinner?"

"How kind you are," Turtle said.

Turtle sat down at the place Anansi had set for him and reached out for a piece of fish. Just as he was about to pop it into his mouth, Anansi spoke up. "Why, Mr. Turtle, don't you know it is bad manners to come to the table with dusty paws? Please go to the stream and wash them."

Turtle, tired and hungry, waddled down the hot-hot hill to the stream.

He washed his paws.

He washed his face. He even washed behind his ears.

Then he waddled back.

Anansi was eating as fast as he could, and most of the food was gone. Turtle sat down and reached for a piece of fish. Just as he was about to pop it into his mouth, Anansi spoke up. "My, my, Mr. Turtle," he said. "Look at those paws. They must have gotten dusty again when you came up the hill. Why don't you go wash them and walk back through the grass."

Turtle was hungrier than ever. But he waddled down to the stream.

He washed his paws as fast as he could and went back up through the grass.

When Turtle got back to the table, Anansi was just scraping the last bits of food from the plate. "What a good dinner that was!" Anansi said. "It is a shame you missed it."

"Yes, it is," said Turtle. "But thank you for asking me. You must come to *my* house for dinner some time."

All the way home Turtle thought, "Anansi *says* all the right things, but *does* all the wrong things. He is mean-mean!"

Now Anansi would never miss a free dinner. So the very next week he went stem by stem through the grass to visit Turtle.

"Well, well," Turtle said. "How good it is to see you. I will go and make our dinner." Turtle dove down into the river with a splash.

His house was all the way at the bottom.

106

Anansi was tired and hungry. He could hardly wait for the delicious dinner Turtle was making. Finally, Turtle came back up eating a juicy clam. "Dinner is ready," he said. Then he dove back down into the river.

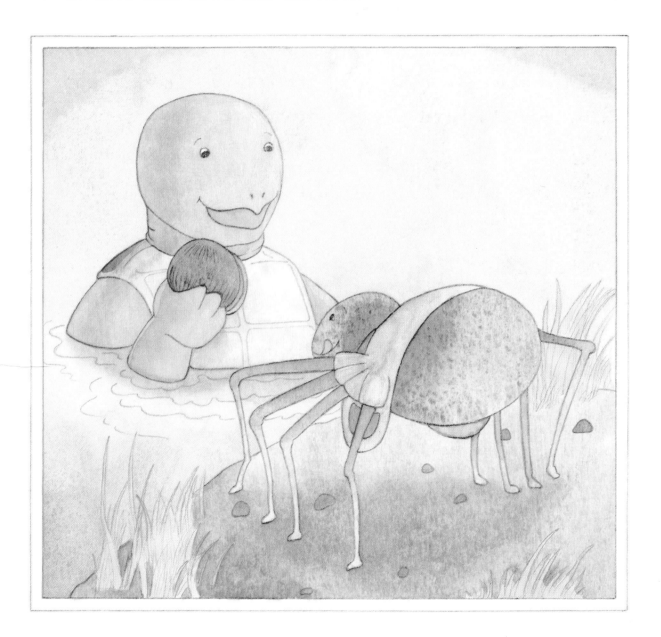

Anansi jumped in after him. But he was so light, he could only float. He flipped and he flopped and he waved his arms wildly, trying to get down to Turtle's house. But none of that worked.

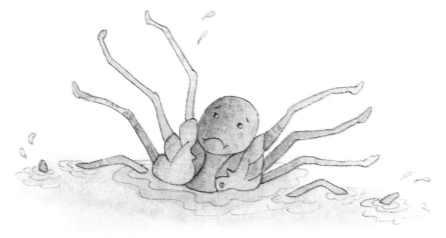

"I know what to do!" he said. He filled his pockets with small round pebbles, then jumped back into the river.

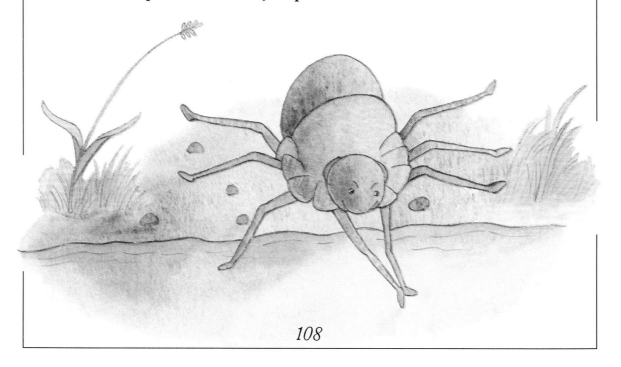

Down, down, down he went and landed with a bump right at Turtle's table.

"What a beautiful dinner you've made!" said Anansi.

"Thank you," said Turtle. "Please help yourself."

Anansi reached out for a clam. Just as he was about to pop it into his mouth, Turtle spoke up. "My goodness, Anansi," he said, "I see you are still wearing your jacket. Don't you know that it is bad manners to leave your jacket on at dinner? Please take it off at once."

Slowly-slowly Anansi took off his jacket. Without the pebbles in his pocket, he was not heavy enough to stay down at the bottom. Slowly-slowly he floated back to the top of the river.

Turtle waved goodbye to Anansi. "Come again soon," he said. And he popped another clam into his mouth.

SYLVESTER
AND THE MAGIC PEBBLE

written and illustrated by William Steig

Sylvester Duncan lived with his mother and father at Acorn Road in Oatsdale. One of his hobbies was collecting pebbles of unusual shape and color.

On a rainy Saturday during vacation he found a quite extraordinary one. It was flaming red, shiny, and perfectly round, like a marble. As he was studying this remarkable pebble, he began to shiver, probably from excitement, and the rain felt cold on his back. "I wish it would stop raining," he said.

To his great surprise the rain stopped. It didn't stop gradually as rains usually do. It CEASED. The drops vanished on the way down, the clouds disappeared, everything was dry, and the sun was shining as if rain had never existed.

In all his young life Sylvester had never had a wish gratified so quickly. It struck him that magic must be at work, and he guessed that the magic must be in the remarkable-looking red pebble. (Where indeed it was.) To make a test, he put the pebble on the ground and said, "I wish it would rain again." Nothing happened. But when he said the same thing holding the pebble in his hoof, the sky turned black, there was lightning and a clap of thunder, and the rain came shooting down.

"What a lucky day this is!" thought Sylvester. "From now on I can have anything I want. My father and mother can have anything they want. My relatives, my friends, and anybody at all can have everything anybody wants!"

He wished the sunshine back in the sky, and he wished a wart on his left hind fetlock would disappear, and it did, and he started home, eager to amaze his father and mother with his magic pebble. He could hardly wait to see their faces. Maybe they wouldn't even believe him at first.

As he was crossing Strawberry Hill, thinking of some of the many, many things he could wish for, he was startled to see a mean, hungry lion looking right at him from behind some tall grass. He was frightened. If he hadn't been so frightened, he could have made the lion disappear, or he could have wished himself safe at home with his father and mother.

He could have wished the lion would turn into a butterfly or a daisy or a gnat. He could have wished many things, but he panicked and couldn't think carefully.

"I wish I were a rock," he said, and he became a rock.

The lion came bounding over, sniffed the rock a hundred times, walked around and around it, and went away confused, perplexed, puzzled, and bewildered. "I saw that little donkey as clear as day. Maybe I'm going crazy," he muttered.

And there was Sylvester, a rock on Strawberry Hill, with the magic pebble lying right beside him on the ground, and he was unable to pick it up. "Oh, how I wish I were myself again," he thought, but nothing happened. He had to be touching the pebble to make the magic work, but there was nothing he could do about it.

His thoughts began to race like mad. He was scared and worried. Being helpless, he felt hopeless. He imagined all the possibilities, and eventually he realized that his only chance of

becoming himself again was for someone to find the red pebble and to wish that the rock next to it would be a donkey. Someone would surely find the red pebble—it was so bright and shiny—but what on earth would make them wish that a rock were a donkey? The chance was one in a billion at best.

Sylvester fell asleep. What else could he do? Night came with many stars.

Meanwhile, back at home, Mr. and Mrs. Duncan paced the floor, frantic with worry. Sylvester had never come home later than dinner time. Where could he be? They stayed up all night wondering what had happened, expecting that Sylvester would surely turn up by morning. But he didn't, of course. Mrs. Duncan cried a lot and Mr. Duncan did his best to soothe her. Both longed to have their dear son with them.

"I will never scold Sylvester as long as I live," said Mrs. Duncan, "no matter what he does."

At dawn, they went about inquiring of all the neighbors.

They talked to all the children—the puppies, the kittens, the colts, the piglets. No one had seen Sylvester since the day before yesterday.

They went to the police. The police could not find their child. All the dogs in Oatsdale went searching for him. They

sniffed behind every rock and tree and blade of grass, into every nook and gully of the neighborhood and beyond, but found not a scent of him. They sniffed the rock on Strawberry Hill, but it smelled like a rock. It didn't smell like Sylvester.

After a month of searching the same places over and over again, and inquiring of the same animals over and over again, Mr. and Mrs. Duncan no longer knew what to do. They concluded that something dreadful must have happened and that they would probably never see their son again. (Though all the time he was less than a mile away.)

They tried their best to be happy, to go about their usual ways. But their usual ways included Sylvester and they were always reminded of him. They were miserable. Life had no meaning for them any more.

Night followed day and day followed night over and over again. Sylvester on the hill woke up less and less often. When he was awake, he was only hopeless and unhappy. He felt he would be a rock forever and he tried to get used to it. He went into an endless sleep. The days grew colder. Fall came with the leaves changing color.
Then the leaves fell and the grass bent to the ground.

Then it was winter. The winds blew, this way and that. It snowed. Mostly, the animals stayed indoors, living on the food they had stored up.

One day a wolf sat on the rock that was Sylvester and howled and howled because he was hungry.

Then the snows melted. The earth warmed up in the spring sun and things budded.

Leaves were on the trees again.
Flowers showed their young faces.

One day in May, Mr. Duncan insisted that his wife go with him on a picnic. "Let's cheer up," he said. "Let us try to live again and be happy even though Sylvester, our angel, is no longer with us." They went to Strawberry Hill.

Mrs. Duncan sat down on the rock. The warmth of his own mother sitting on him woke Sylvester up from his deep winter sleep. How he wanted to shout, "Mother! Father! It's me, Sylvester, I'm right here!" But he couldn't talk. He had no voice. He was stone-dumb.

Mr. Duncan walked aimlessly about while Mrs. Duncan set out the picnic food on the rock—alfalfa sandwiches, pickled

oats, sassafras salad, timothy compote. Suddenly Mr. Duncan saw the red pebble. "What a fantastic pebble!" he exclaimed. "Sylvester would have loved it for his collection." He put the pebble on the rock.

They sat down to eat. Sylvester was now as wide awake as a donkey that was a rock could possibly be. Mrs. Duncan felt some mysterious excitement. "You know, Father," she said suddenly, "I have the strangest feeling that our dear Sylvester is still alive and not far away."

"I am, I am!" Sylvester wanted to shout, but he couldn't. If only he had realized that the pebble resting on his back was the magic pebble!

"Oh, how I wish he were here with us on this lovely May day," said Mrs. Duncan. Mr. Duncan looked sadly at the ground. "Don't you wish it too, Father?" she said. He looked at her as if to say, "How can you ask such a question?"

Mr. and Mrs. Duncan looked at each other with great sorrow.

"I wish I were myself again, I wish I were my real self again!" thought Sylvester.

And in less than an instant, he was!

132

You can imagine the scene that followed—the embraces, the kisses, the questions, the answers, the loving looks, and the fond exclamations!

When they had eventually calmed down a bit, and had gotten home, Mr. Duncan put the magic pebble in an iron safe. Some day they might want to use it, but really, for now, what more could they wish for? They all had all that they wanted.

THE GINGERBREAD MAN

Once upon a time there was an old woman who lived by herself in a cottage. One day she decided to make a gingerbread man. She mixed the batter and shaped the man just right. Then she popped it into the oven to bake.

When the Gingerbread Man was ready, the old woman
opened the oven door. As soon as she did, the Gingerbread
Man jumped up and ran out of the house.

"Stop!" cried the old woman.

But the Gingerbread Man did not stop. He ran down the road.

The old woman ran after him. The Gingerbread Man laughed and said:

"Run, Woman, run as fast as you can
But you won't catch me—
I'm the Gingerbread Man!"

The Gingerbread Man turned a corner and met a Farmer. When the Farmer saw the Old Woman running after the Gingerbread Man, he started to run after him, too.

"I ran faster than the Old Woman, and I can run faster than you, too," said the Gingerbread Man.

"Is that so?" said the Farmer.

The Gingerbread Man laughed and said:

"Run, Farmer, run as fast as you can
But you won't catch me—
I'm the Gingerbread Man!"

At the bottom of the hill, the Gingerbread Man ran into the Farmer's two children.

"It's a race!" they said.

"That's right!" said the Gingerbread Man. "I ran faster than the Old Woman and faster than the Farmer, and I can run faster than you, too!"

"Oh, no you can't!" said the Children.

The Gingerbread Man laughed and said:

"Run, Children, run as fast as you can
But you won't catch me—
I'm the Gingerbread Man!"

Next the Gingerbread Man met the Farmer's dog.

"This race looks like fun!" said the Dog. "And if I catch you, I eat you!"

"But remember," said the Gingerbread Man, "I ran faster than the Old Woman and faster than the Farmer and faster than the Children, and I can run faster than you, too!"

"We'll see about that!" said the Dog.

The Gingerbread Man laughed and said:

"Run, Dog, run as fast as you can
But you won't catch me—
I'm the Gingerbread Man!"

The Gingerbread Man was way ahead of the others when he met a fox.

"You're a fast runner!" said the Fox.

"Yes, I am," said the Gingerbread Man. "I ran faster than the Old Woman and faster than the Farmer and faster than the Children and faster than the Dog, and I can run faster than you, too!"

"What was that?" said the Fox. "I couldn't hear you."

For the first time since he ran away from the Old Woman, the Gingerbread Man stopped. He said a little louder than before, "I RAN FASTER THAN THE OLD WOMAN AND FASTER THAN THE FARMER AND FASTER THAN THE CHILDREN AND FASTER THAN THE DOG AND I CAN RUN FASTER THAN YOU, TOO!"

"Can you come a little closer?" said the Fox. "I still can't hear you."

The Gingerbread Man went a little closer and said even louder than before, "I RAN FASTER THAN THE OLD WOMAN AND FASTER THAN THE FARMER AND FASTER THAN THE CHILDREN AND FASTER THAN THE DOG, AND I CAN RUN FASTER THAN YOU, TOO!"

"If you'd come just a little closer," said the Fox, "I'm sure I could hear you then."

The Gingerbread Man went a little closer. He put his face right up to the Fox's ear and shouted, "I RAN FASTER THAN THE OLD WOMAN AND FASTER THAN THE FARMER AND FASTER THAN THE CHILDREN AND FASTER THAN THE DOG AND I CAN RUN FASTER THAN YOU, TOO!"

"Oh, can you?" said the Fox.

Then he opened his mouth and—snip, snap!—gobbled the Gingerbread Man before there was time for an answer!

THE THREE LITTLE PIGS

Once upon a time three little pigs set out to make their way in the world.

"Beware the big, bad wolf," said their mother.

The first little pig had not gone far when he met a man with a bundle of straw.

"Please, man, give me some straw so that I can build a house," said the first little pig.

The man did, and the pig built a house of straw.

Soon the big, bad wolf came along and knocked on the door.

"Little pig, little pig, let me come in," said the wolf.

"No, no, not by the hair of my chinny chin chin," cried the little pig.

The wolf answered, "Then I'll huff and I'll puff and I'll blow your house in."

So he huffed and he puffed and he blew the house in, and he ate up the first little pig.

The second little pig was walking along when he met a man with a bundle of sticks.

"Please, man, give me some sticks so that I can build a house," said the second little pig.

The man did, and the pig built a house of sticks.

Soon the big bad wolf came along and knocked on the door.

"Little pig, little pig, let me come in," said the wolf.

"No, no, not by the hair of my chinny chin chin," said the little pig.

The wolf answered, "Then I'll huff and I'll puff and I'll blow your house in!"

So he huffed and he puffed and he blew the house in, and he ate up the second little pig.

The third little pig was walking along when he met a man with a load of bricks.

"Please, man, give me some bricks so that I can build a house," said the third little pig.

The man did, and the pig built a house of bricks.

Soon the big bad wolf came along and said, "Little pig, little pig, let me come in."

"No, no, not by the hair of my chinny chin chin," answered the pig.

The wolf answered, "Then I'll huff and I'll puff and I'll blow your house in!"

So he huffed and he puffed,

and he huffed and he puffed,

and he huffed and he puffed.

But he could *not* blow that house down.

"Little pig," said the wolf. "I know where there is a field of tasty turnips."

"Where?" asked the pig.

"Over in Mr. Smith's field. Be ready tomorrow at six o'clock and we'll get some dinner," said the wolf.

Well the little pig got up at five o'clock. He went to the field, got the turnips, and returned home before the wolf came.

"Little pig, are you ready?" called the wolf.

"Ready?" said the pig. "Why, I've been and come back again!"

Well, the wolf was very angry, but he said, "Little pig, I know where there's a nice apple tree."

"Where?" said the pig.

"Over in Merry-Garden," said the wolf. "Be ready at five o'clock tomorrow, and we'll get some apples."

Well, the pig got up at four o'clock and went off for apples. But just as he climbed up the tree, there was the wolf coming.

"Little pig, are you here already?" said the wolf.

"Yes," said the pig. "The apples are delicious. Here, I'll throw you down one."

And he threw an apple very far, so the wolf had to run a long way to pick it up.

Then the little pig jumped down and ran home.

The next day the wolf came and said, "Little pig, are you going to the fair tomorrow?"

"Yes, I will go," said the pig. "What time will you come for me?"

"At three o'clock," said the wolf.

Well, the pig went early, as usual, and bought a butter churn at the fair. He was walking down the road with it, when he saw the wolf coming.

The little pig got into the churn to hide, and the churn rolled down the hill with him in it, which frightened the wolf so much that he ran away.

The wolf went to the pig's house and told him how he had been frightened by a great round thing that had rolled down the hill at him.

"That was me in a butter churn," said the pig.

Then the wolf was very angry indeed, and started to come down the chimney to eat the little pig. But the pig was ready for him. He had a great kettle of water on the fire, and when the wolf came down, he fell in. Then the pig put the cover on the kettle, boiled up the wolf, and had him for supper. And so the little pig lived happily ever afterward.

ANGUS AND THE CAT

Told and Pictured by Marjorie Flack

Each day as Angus grew older he grew longer but not much higher. Scottie dogs grow that way.

Now as Angus grew older and longer he learned MANY THINGS. He learned it is best to stay in one's own yard   and

FROGS can jump   but

NOT to jump after them   and

BALLOONS go

POP!

Angus also learned NOT to lie on the sofa and NOT to take SOMEBODY ELSE'S food and things like that.

But there was SOMETHING outdoors Angus was very curious about but had NEVER learned about, and that was

CATS.   The leash was TOO short.

Until one day WHAT should Angus find INDOORS lying on the SOFA but a strange little CAT!

Angus came closer– The CAT sat up. Angus came closer–

Up jumped the CAT onto the arm of the sofa. Angus came closer and—

SISS-S-S-S-S-S!!! That little CAT boxed Angus's ears!

Woo-oo-oof—Woo-oo-oof! said Angus.

Up jumped the CAT onto the sofa back, up to the mantel
—and Angus was not high enough to reach her!

But at lunch time down she came to try and take Angus's food—though not for long.

Up she jumped onto the table, and Angus was not high enough to reach her!

At nap time there she was sitting in Angus's own special square of sunshine–WASHING HER FACE, though not for long.

Up she jumped onto the window sill, and Angus was not high enough to reach her!

For THREE whole days Angus was very busy chasing THAT CAT, but she always went up out of reach until on the fourth day he chased her UP-THE-STAIRS

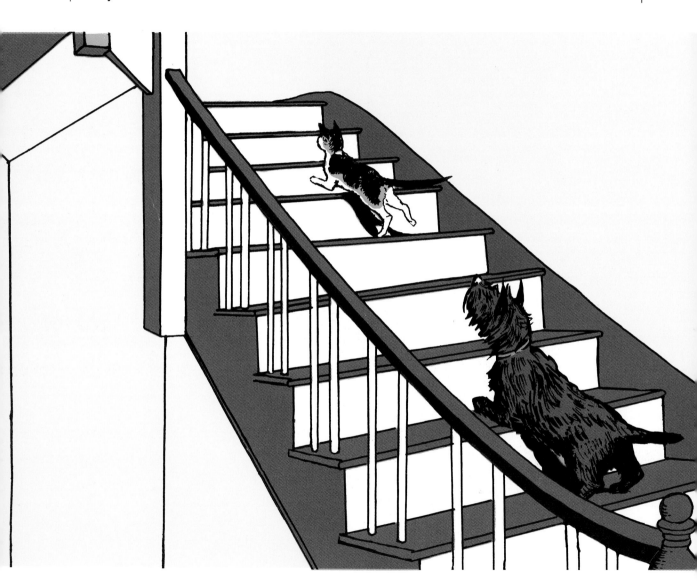

into the BEDROOM and she was completely GONE!
Angus looked under the bed—no CAT was there.

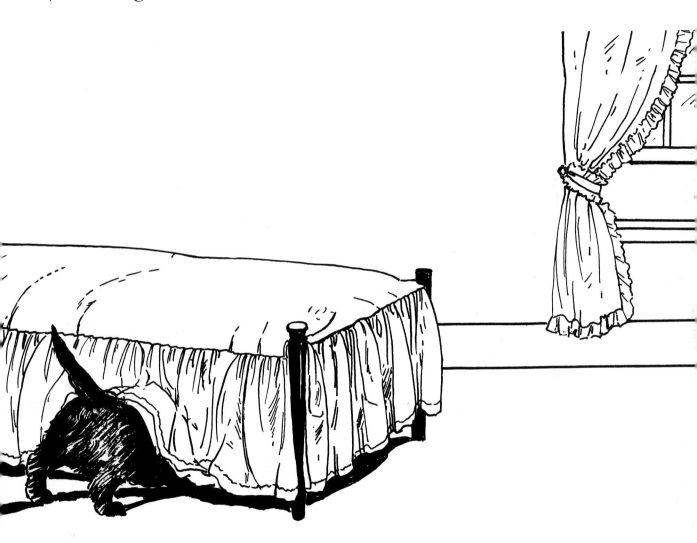

Angus looked out the window into his yard,

into the next yard—no CAT could he see ANYWHERE.

Angus went DOWN-THE-STAIRS. He looked on the sofa—
no CAT was there. He looked on the mantel—no CAT
was there. Angus looked on the table and on the window sills—
no CAT was indoors ANYWHERE.

So Angus was ALL-ALONE. There was no CAT to box his ears. There was no CAT to take his food. There was no CAT to sit in his sunshine. There was no CAT to chase away. So Angus was ALL-ALONE and he had NOTHING-TO-DO!

Angus missed the little CAT.

But—at lunch time he heard this noise: P U R R R R R —

and there she was again. And Angus knew and the CAT knew that Angus knew that—

Angus was GLAD the cat came back!

THE MAN WHO DIDN'T WASH HIS DISHES

by Phyllis Krasilovsky

There once was a man who lived alone in a little house on the edge of a town. He didn't have any wife or children, so he always cooked his own supper, cleaned the house by himself, and made his own bed.

One night he came home hungrier than usual, so he made himself a big, big supper. It was a very good supper (he liked to cook and could make good things to eat), but there was so much of it that he grew very, very tired by the time he'd finished. He just sat back in his chair, as full as he could be, and decided he'd leave the dishes till the next night, and then he would wash them all at once.

But the next night he was TWICE as hungry, so he cooked
TWICE as big a supper, and took TWICE as long to eat it,
and was TWICE as tired by the time he'd finished. So he left
THOSE dishes in the sink, too.

Well, as the days went by he got hungrier and hungrier, and more and more tired, and so he never washed his dishes. After a while there were so MANY dirty dishes that they didn't all fit in the sink. So he began to pile them on the table.

Soon the table was so full that he began to put them on his bookshelves. And when THEY were full, he put them just everywhere he could find an empty place. Soon he had them all piled on the floor, too. In fact, the floor got to be so FULL of dishes that he had a hard time getting into his house at night—THEY WERE EVEN PILED AGAINST THE DOOR!

Then one night he looked in his closet and found that there WASN'T ONE CLEAN DISH LEFT! He was hungry enough to eat out of anything, so he ate out of the soap dish from the bathroom.

It was too dirty for him to use again the NEXT night, so he used one of his ash trays. Pretty soon he had used up all his ash trays.

THEN he ate out of some clean flowerpots he found down the cellar. When THEY were all used up, he ate out of his candy dishes and drank water from vases.

He used up EVERYTHING finally—even the pots he cooked his food in, and he didn't know what to do! He was SOOOO unhappy. His whole house was full of dirty dishes—and dirty flowerpots—and dirty ash trays—and dirty candy dishes—and dirty pots—and a dirty soap dish. He couldn't even find his books—or his alarm clock—or even his BED any more! He couldn't sit down to think because even his chairs were filled with dishes, and he couldn't find the sink so he could wash them!

But THEN—all of a sudden—IT BEGAN TO RAIN! And the man got an idea. He drove his big truck around to the side of the house and piled all the dishes—and all the vases—and all the flowerpots—and all the ash trays—and all the candy dishes—and the soap dish—on it, and drove the truck out into the rain.

The rain fell on everything and soon they were clean again.
THE RAIN HAD WASHED THEM!

Then the man carried everything back into the house again. He put the dishes in the dish closet, the pots in the pot closet, the ash trays on the tables, the candy dishes on the shelves, the flowerpots in the cellar, the vases where the vases go, and the soap dish in the bathroom. He was so very, very tired after carrying everything back and putting it away that he decided that from then on he would always wash his dishes just as soon as he had finished his supper.

The next night when he came home he cooked his supper, and—when he had finished eating it—he washed the dishes and put them right away. He did this every night after that, too. He is very happy now. He can find his chairs, and he can find his alarm clock, and he can find his BED. It is easy for him to get into his house, too, because there are no more dishes piled on the floor—or anywhere!

THE LION AND THE MOUSE

An Aesop Fable

retold by Stephanie Calmenson

Lion had been hunting all morning and was tired. He lay down in the cool grass to rest, not wanting to be disturbed. But as soon as he closed his eyes, he felt something tippy-toeing up his back.

It was a tiny, gray mouse. Lion lay as still as a rock, which is just what Mouse thought she was upon. Soon she would know better. For each step she took brought her closer to Lion's strong jaws and quick paws.

SNAP! "I've got you!" roared Lion as he whisked Mouse up by her tail. He was about to pop Mouse into his huge, hungry mouth when he heard her beg, "Please, forgive me! I did not mean to disturb you. If you will let me go this time, you can be certain I will return your kindness one day."

Lion laughed. "What could a tiny thing like you ever do for me?"

"I cannot say for sure," said Mouse. "But I promise you won't be sorry."

Lion flicked the mouse away. "You're too little to bother with anyway," he said.

A few days later, some hunters caught Lion and tied him to a tree. Mouse heard Lion's furious roar and ran to him. She quickly began gnawing through the ropes that bound him. It took some time, but finally she set Lion free.

"Thank you," said Lion. "Not only have you freed me, you have taught me a lesson worth remembering."

EVEN A SMALL FRIEND MAY BE A GREAT FRIEND.

CORDUROY

written and illustrated by Don Freeman

Corduroy is a bear who once lived in the toy department of a big store. Day after day he waited with all the other animals and dolls for somebody to come along and take him home.
The store was always filled with shoppers buying all sorts of things, but no one ever seemed to want a small bear in green overalls.
Then one morning a little girl stopped and looked straight into Corduroy's bright eyes.

"Oh, Mommy!" she said. "Look! There's the very bear I've always
wanted."

"Not today, dear." Her mother sighed. "I've spent too much already.
Besides, he doesn't look new. He's lost the button to one of his
shoulder straps."

Corduroy watched them sadly as they walked away.

"I didn't know I'd lost a button," he said to himself. "Tonight I'll go
and see if I can find it."

Late that evening, when all the shoppers had gone and the doors were shut and locked, Corduroy climbed carefully down from his shelf and began searching everywhere on the floor for his lost button.

Suddenly he felt the floor moving under him! Quite by accident he had stepped onto an escalator—and up he went!

"Could this be a mountain?" he wondered. "I think I've always wanted to climb a mountain."

He stepped off the escalator as it reached the next floor, and there,
before his eyes, was a most amazing sight—
tables and chairs and lamps and sofas, and rows and rows of beds.
"This must be a palace!" Corduroy gasped. "I guess I've always

wanted to live in a palace."
He wandered around admiring the furniture.
"This must be a bed," he said. "I've always wanted to sleep in a bed." And up he crawled onto a large, thick mattress.

All at once he saw something small and round.

"Why, here's my button!" he cried. And he tried to pick it up. But, like all the other buttons on the mattress, it was tied down tight.

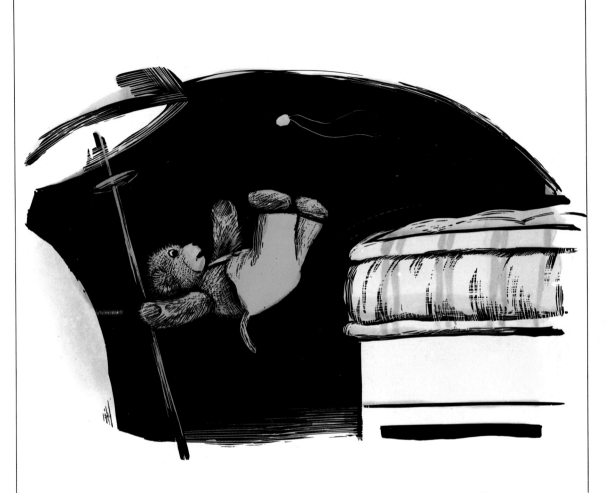

He yanked and pulled with both paws until POP! Off came the
button—and off the mattress Corduroy toppled,
bang into a tall floor lamp. Over it fell with a crash!

Corduroy didn't know it, but there was someone else awake in the store. The night watchman was going his rounds on the floor above. When he heard the crash he came dashing down the escalator. "Now who in the world did that!" he exclaimed. "Somebody must be hiding around here!"

He flashed his light under and over sofas and beds until he came to
the biggest bed of all. And there he saw two fuzzy brown ears
sticking up from under the cover.

"Hello!" he said. "How did *you* get upstairs?"

The watchman tucked Corduroy under his arm and carried him
down the escalator and set him on the shelf in the toy
department with the other animals and dolls.

Corduroy was just waking up when the first customers came into the store in the morning. And there, looking at him with a wide, warm smile, was the same little girl he'd seen only the day before. "I'm Lisa," she said, "and you're going to be my very own bear. Last night I counted what I've saved in my piggy bank and my mother said I could bring you home."

"Shall I put him in a box for you?" the saleslady asked.

"Oh, no thank you," Lisa answered. And she carried Corduroy home in her arms.

She ran all the way up four flights of stairs, into her family's apartment, and straight to her own room.

Corduroy blinked. There was a chair and a chest of drawers, and alongside a girl-size bed stood a little bed just the right size for him. The room was small, nothing like that enormous palace in the department store.

"This must be home," he said. "I *know* I've always wanted a home!"

Lisa sat down with Corduroy on her lap and began to sew a button on his overalls.

"I like you the way you are," she said, "but you'll be more comfortable with your shoulder strap fastened."

"You must be a friend," said Corduroy. "I've always wanted a friend."

"Me too!" said Lisa, and gave him a big hug.

VERY TALL MOUSE
AND VERY SHORT MOUSE

written and illustrated by Arnold Lobel

Once there was a very tall mouse
and a very short mouse
who were good friends.

When they met,
Very Tall Mouse would say,
"Hello, Very Short Mouse."
And Very Short Mouse would say,
"Hello, Very Tall Mouse."

The two friends would often
take walks together.
As they walked along,
Very Tall Mouse would say,
"Hello birds."
And Very Short Mouse would say,
"Hello bugs."

When they
passed by a garden
Very Tall Mouse would say,
"Hello flowers."
And Very Short Mouse
would say,
"Hello roots."

When they passed by a house,
Very Tall Mouse would say,
"Hello roof."
And Very Short Mouse
would say,
"Hello cellar."

One day the two mice
were caught in a storm.
Very Tall Mouse said,
"Hello raindrops."
And Very Short Mouse said,
"Hello puddles."

They ran indoors to get dry.
"Hello ceiling,"
said Very Tall Mouse.
"Hello floor,"
said Very Short Mouse.

Soon the storm was over.
The two friends
ran to the window.

Very Tall Mouse held
Very Short Mouse up to see.
"Hello rainbow!"
they both said together.

GOLDILOCKS AND THE THREE BEARS

Once upon a time there were three bears who lived together in a little house in the woods. There was a Great Big Bear, a Middle-Sized bear, and a Wee Little Bear.

Each bear had a bowl for his porridge. The Great Big Bear had a great big bowl. The Middle-Sized Bear had a middle-sized bowl. And the Wee Little Bear had a wee little bowl.

Each bear had a chair to sit in. There was a great big chair for the Great Big Bear, a middle-sized chair for the Middle-Sized Bear, and a wee little chair for the Wee Little Bear.

And each bear had a bed to sleep in. The Great Big Bear had a great big bed. The Middle-Sized Bear had a middle-sized bed. And the Wee Little Bear had a wee little bed.

Every morning the Bears liked to eat porridge for breakfast. One morning, when the porridge was too hot to eat, they decided to go for a walk in the woods.

While they were gone a little girl named Goldilocks came to their house. Goldilocks peeked through the window. She saw no one inside. So she knocked on the door. When no one answered, she opened the door and went in.

The first thing Goldilocks saw were the three bowls of porridge. She was so hungry, she decided to eat some.

First she tasted the porridge in the great big bowl. But it was too hot.

Then she tasted the porridge in the middle-sized bowl. But it was too cold.

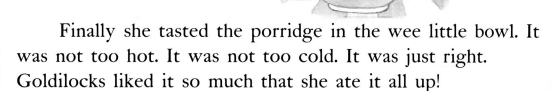

Finally she tasted the porridge in the wee little bowl. It was not too hot. It was not too cold. It was just right. Goldilocks liked it so much that she ate it all up!

Then Goldilocks went into the next room. She saw the three chairs and decided to sit and rest awhile.

First she sat in the chair of the Great Big Bear. It was too high.

Then she sat in chair of the Middle-Sized Bear. It was too wide.

So, Goldilocks sat in the chair of Wee Little Baby Bear. It was not too high. It was not too wide. It was just right.

But with Goldilocks in it, the chair broke all to pieces!

Next, Goldilocks went to the bedroom. She saw the three beds and being very tired she decided to take a nap.

First she lay down on the bed of the Great Big Bear. It was too hard.

Then she lay down on the bed of the Middle-Sized Bear. It was too soft.

At last Goldilocks lay down on the bed of the Wee Little Bear. It was not too hard. It was not too soft. It was just right. So Goldilocks fell fast asleep.

Soon, The Three Bears came home. They were hungry for porridge after their long walk. The Great Big Bear took one look in his bowl and growled in his great big voice, "SOMEONE HAS BEEN TASTING MY PORRIDGE!"

The Middle-Sized Bear looked in her bowl and said in her middle-sized voice, "SOMEONE HAS BEEN TASTING *my* PORRIDGE!"

Then the Wee Little Bear looked in his bowl and said in his wee little voice, "Someone has been tasting my porridge and has eaten it all up!"

The Three Bears hurried to the next room. The Great Big Bear took one look at his chair and growled in his great big voice, "SOMEONE HAS BEEN SITTING IN MY CHAIR!"

The Middle-Sized Bear looked at her chair and said in her middle-sized voice, "SOMEONE HAS BEEN SITTING IN *my* CHAIR!"

Then the Wee Little Bear looked at his chair and cried in his wee little voice, "Someone has been sitting in my chair and has broken it all to pieces!"

The Three Bears went to the bedroom. The Great Big Bear took one look at his bed and growled in his great big voice, "SOMEONE HAS BEEN SLEEPING IN MY BED!"

The Middle-Sized Bear looked at her bed and said in her middle-sized voice, "SOMEONE HAS BEEN SLEEPING IN *my* BED!"

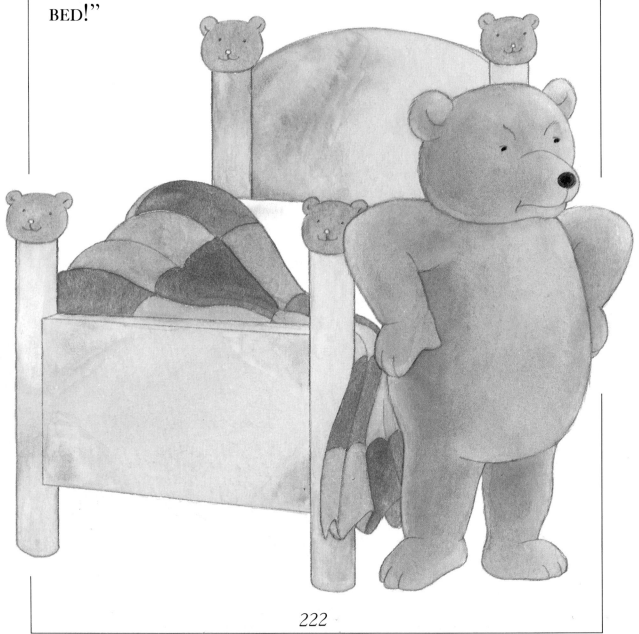

Then the Wee Little Bear looked at his bed and cried in his wee little voice, "Someone has been sleeping in my bed and here she is!"

FINGERPLAYS

AIRPORT

Sally Lucas

Here is the tower.

Here is the plane.

Here is the pilot.

Here is the rain.

226

"Pilot to tower."

"Tower to plane!"

Come in for a landing.

Watch out for the rain."

227

THE PEANUT SONG

Oh, a peanut sat
On a railroad track,

His heart was all a-flutter.

Along came the five-fifteen,

Uh-oh, peanut butter!

228

THE ELEPHANT

The elephant goes like this and that.

He's terrible big.
And he's terrible fat.

He has no fingers.
And he has no toes.

But goodness gracious, what a nose!

ALI GATOR AND ANNIE GATOR SAY THE ALPHABET

Can you say your abc's?

HERE, PUPPY!
A Counting Story

Can you count with Puppy?

"Here, Puppy!" Puppy heard his little girl call.
Puppy went to find her.

On the way he stopped to look at:

1 golden butterfly   2 fuzzy caterpillars

3 chirping birds   4 friendly children

5 frisky kittens

6 quacking ducks

7 croaking frogs

8 pretty sailboats

9 yellow daisies

10 big balloons

Finally Puppy found his little girl.
"What a good puppy you are!" she said.

CIRCUS COLORS

Can you find these colors in the circus?

Red   Yellow   Blue   Green

Orange Purple Pink Brown

ALI GATOR AND ANNIE GATOR IN SHAPE CITY

Can you find these shapes in the picture?

 Circle  Square  Triangle  Rectangle

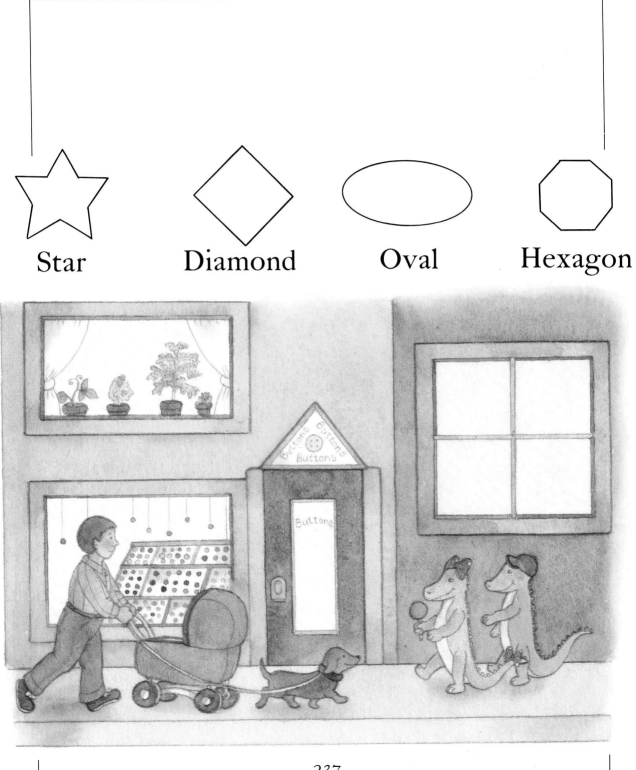

Star Diamond Oval Hexagon

THE FOUR SEASONS

There are four seasons in every year.
Do you know their names?

In WINTER glide on ice and snow.

In SPRING see grass and flowers grow.

In SUMMER feel an ocean breeze.

In FALL watch leaves fall from the trees.

ALI GATOR AND ANNIE GATOR IN OPPOSITES ALL!

Do you know
Fast and slow?

Up and down,

Smile and frown.

Fat and thin,

Out and in.

Short and tall,

Big and small.

Opposites all!

STOP, MONKEY, STOP!
A Rebus

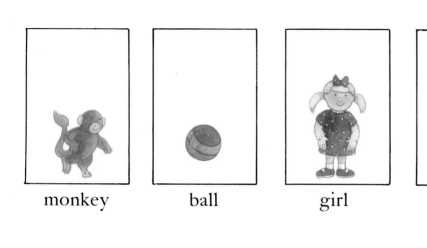

monkey   ball   girl   hat

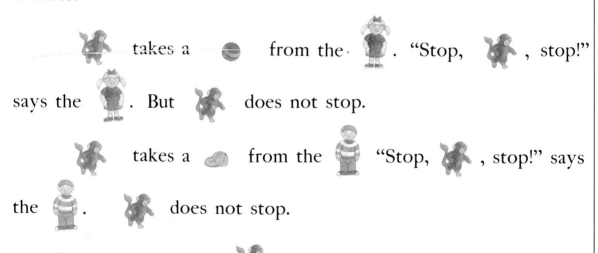

Here comes 🐵 . He likes to have fun. But he gets into trouble.

🐵 takes a ⚫ from the 👧 . "Stop, 🐵 , stop!" says the 👧 . But 🐵 does not stop.

🐵 takes a 🧢 from the 🧒 "Stop, 🐵 , stop!" says the 🧒 . 🐵 does not stop.

Look what that bad 🐵 does now! He takes a 🚗 from the 👤 . The man says, "Stop, 🐵 , stop!" But 🐵 cannot

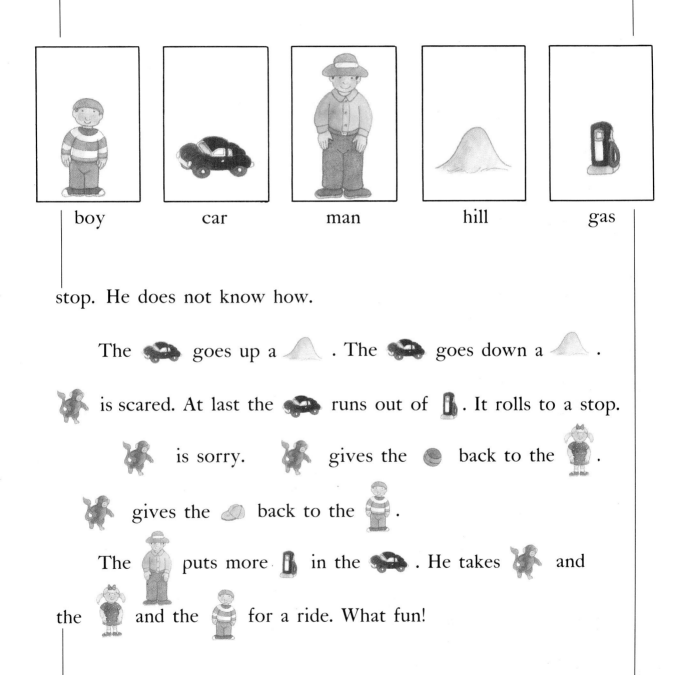

boy   car   man   hill   gas

stop. He does not know how.

The 🚗 goes up a ⛰ . The 🚗 goes down a ⛰ . 🐒 is scared. At last the 🚗 runs out of ⛽ . It rolls to a stop.

🐒 is sorry. 🐒 gives the ⚫ back to the 👧 .

🐒 gives the 🧢 back to the 👦 .

The 👨 puts more ⛽ in the 🚗 . He takes 🐒 and the 👧 and the 👦 for a ride. What fun!

ALI GATOR AND ANNIE GATOR IN ROLLER SKATES
A Wordless Story

Look at the pictures. Tell the story out loud.

1.

2.

3.

4.

5.

6.

7.

8.

9.

10.

Can You Find It?

I can't find it—not at all.
Do you see my yellow ball?

Do you see my teddy bear?
I can't find him anywhere.

We don't see our picture book.
You can find it if you look.

Help us find our dinosaur.
Did we leave it on the floor?

I've looked underneath my bed.
But I still can't find my sled.
Do *you* see it?

I have one. I should have two.
Can you find my other shoe?

We have lost our dog and cat.
Can you help us out with that?
Do you see them?

I've been hunting near and far
For my big banana car.

I used to a have a green toy elf.
But it isn't on the shelf.
Can you find it?

TITLE INDEX

AUTHOR AND ARTIST INDEX

FIRST LINE INDEX

JOANNA COLE has taught elementary school, has worked for a news magazine, and for several years was a senior editor for children's books. Today she is a full-time author, writing for and about children. Many of her more than two dozen children's books have been selected by the American Library Association as Notable Books. She has compiled three anthologies, *Best-Loved Folktales of the World*, *A New Treasury of Children's Poetry*, and, with Stephanie Calmenson, *The Laugh Book: A New Treasury of Humor for Children*. She is married, has a daughter, Rachel, and lives in New York City.

STEPHANIE CALMENSON is the author of many books for children, including *What Am I?: Very First Riddles* and *The Children's Aesop: Selected Fables*. She is also the compiler, with Joanna Cole, of *The Laugh Book: A New Treasury of Humor for Children*. Before turning to writing full-time, she was an elementary school teacher, a children's book editor, and editorial director of *Parents Magazine*'s Read-Aloud Book Club for Children. She grew up in Brooklyn, New York, and now lives in Manhattan.

ANN SCHWENINGER, a native of Colorado, received her Bachelor of Fine Arts degree from the California Institute of the Arts in Valencia. She studied the illustration and writing of children's books with Uri Shulevitz in New York City. She has written and illustrated six books, including *Christmas Secrets*, *Halloween Surprises*, and *Birthday Wishes*, and illustrated twenty-four, most recently *Mother Goose and Other Nursery Rhymes* and *Thump and Plunk* by Janice Udry. Ms. Schweninger lives in New York City.